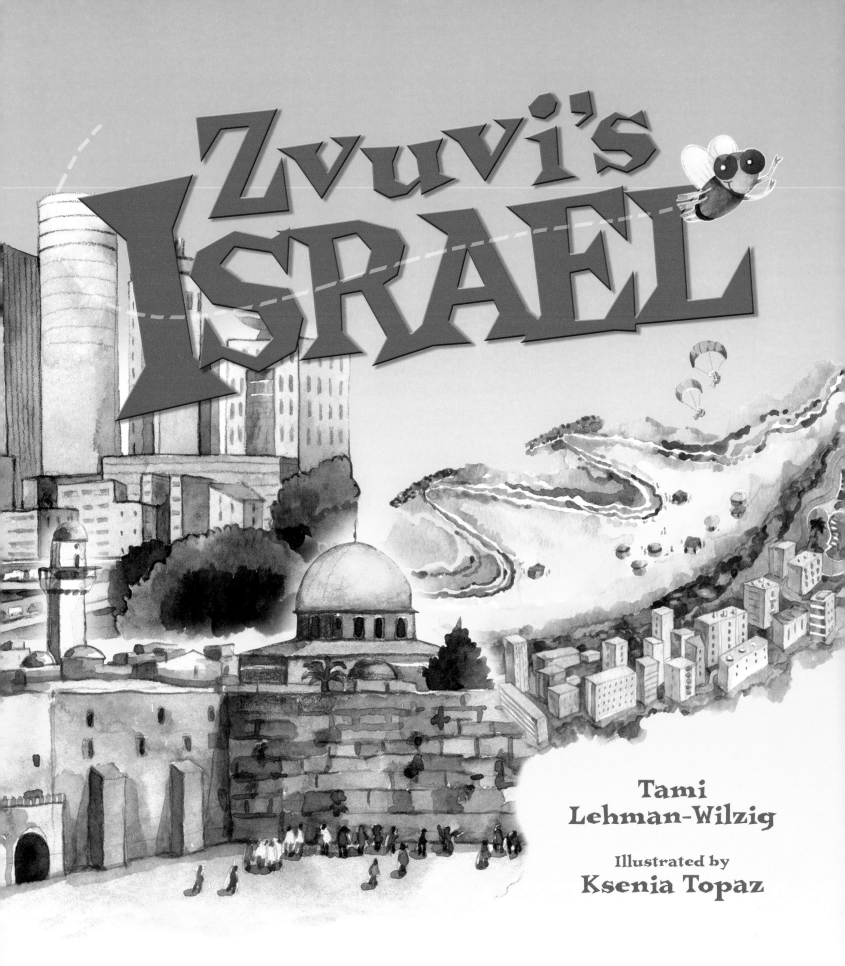

# Zvuvi's ISRAEL

Tami
Lehman-Wilzig

Illustrated by
Ksenia Topaz

KAR-BEN
PUBLISHING

To Sam with love. Thank you for letting me make Israel our home. –T.L.W.

To my amazing daughters, who always stand by me, both as family
and as the most trusted reviewers of my work. –K.T.

# GLOSSARY

**Bar Mitzvah** – coming of age ceremony for Jewish boy at age 13

**Druze** – An independent religious community living in Israel whose
tradition blends Islam and other philosophies

**Elijah** – Jewish prophet

**Felafel** – Sandwich made of fried chickpea balls stuffed in pita

**Hanukkah** – Winter holiday celebrating the victory of the Jews
over the Syrians in 132 BCE

**Labriut** – "To your health" in Hebrew, comment to a person
who sneezes

**Matkot** – Ping pong-like game played on Israel's beaches

**Shofar** – Ram's horn blown on the Jewish New Year

**Torah** – Scroll containing the Five Books of Moses

KAR-BEN PUBLISHING
A division of Lerner Publishing Group, Inc.
241 First Avenue North
Minneapolis, MN 55401 U.S.A.
1-800-4-Karben

Website address: www.karben.com

Library of Congress Cataloging-in-Publication Data

Lehman-Wilzig, Tami.
   Zvuvi's Israel / by Tami Lehman-Wilzig ; illustrated by Ksenia Topaz.
       p.  cm.
   Summary: Zvuvi, an enthusiastic fly, takes his cousin Zahava—and the
reader—on a fast-paced tour of Israel.
   ISBN 978–0–8225–8759–0 (lib. bdg. : alk. paper)
   1. Israel—Juvenile fiction. [1. Israel—Fiction. 2. Flies—Fiction.
3. Cousins—Fiction. 4. Jews—Israel—Fiction.] I. Topaz, Ksenia, ill. II. Title.
PZ7.L53223Zvu 2009
[E]—dc22                                                    2007048346

Manufactured in the United States of America
1 2 3 4 5 – DP – 14 13 12 11 10 09

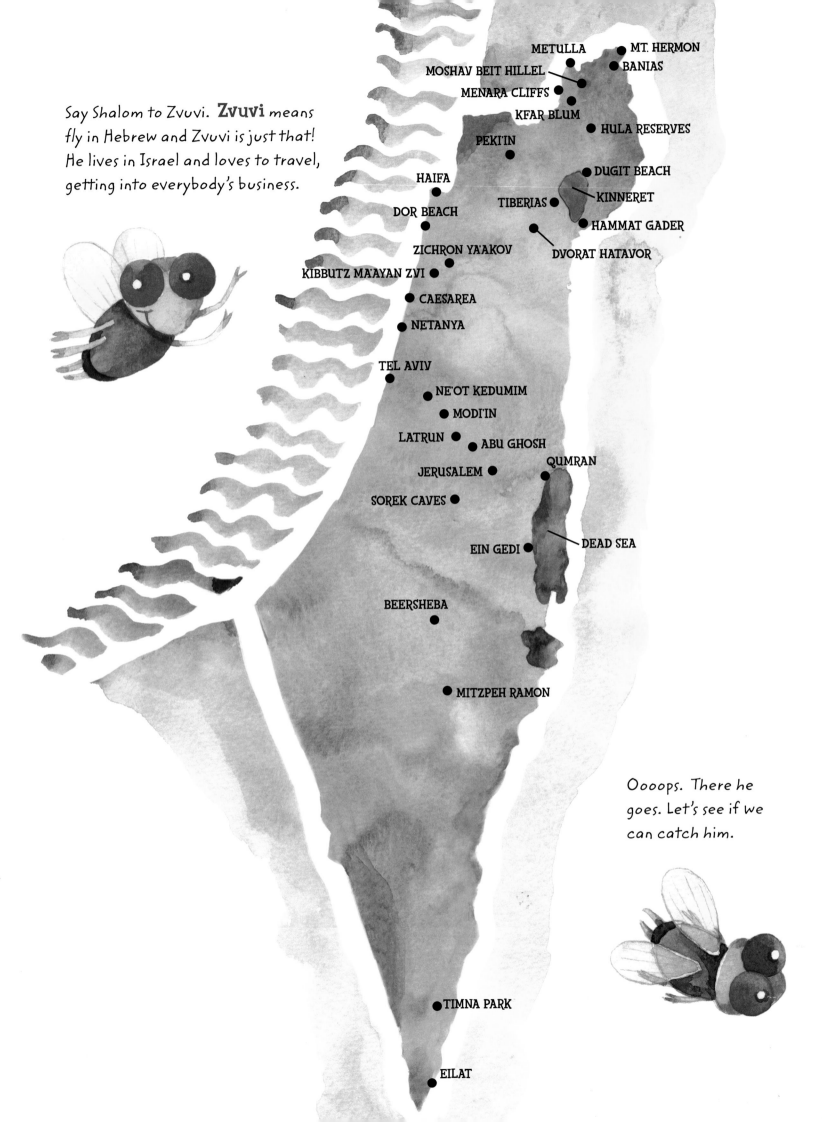

Say Shalom to Zvuvi. **Zvuvi** means fly in Hebrew and Zvuvi is just that! He lives in Israel and loves to travel, getting into everybody's business.

METULLA

MT. HERMON

MOSHAV BEIT HILLEL

BANIAS

MENARA CLIFFS

KFAR BLUM

HULA RESERVES

PEKI'IN

DUGIT BEACH

HAIFA

KINNERET

DOR BEACH

TIBERIAS

HAMMAT GADER

ZICHRON YA'AKOV

DVORAT HATAVOR

KIBBUTZ MA'AYAN ZVI

CAESAREA

NETANYA

TEL AVIV

NE'OT KEDUMIM

MODI'IN

LATRUN

ABU GHOSH

QUMRAN

JERUSALEM

SOREK CAVES

DEAD SEA

EIN GEDI

BEERSHEBA

MITZPEH RAMON

Oooops. There he goes. Let's see if we can catch him.

TIMNA PARK

EILAT

# A "Wail" of a Time in Jerusalem

Zvuvi meets cousin Zahava at the **Kotel, the Wailing Wall.** Lots of people come here to pray. She is tucking her prayer between the big stones. "It's a secret," she whispers.

A Bar Mitzvah boy is reading from the Torah. When he finishes, people shower him with candy.

Careful, Zvuvi! He ducks just in time.

Zahava and Zvuvi zoom out of the Old City through the **Jaffa Gate** to begin their tour of Jerusalem.

"Wow! A giant upside down mushroom!" Zvuvi says, as they fly over the Israel Museum.

"It's the **Shrine of the Book.** It has old scrolls discovered at the Dead Sea," Zahava tells him.

"And there's a model of the **Holy Temple** . . . just like it looked thousands of years ago."

"Lunch time," says Zvuvi, nibbling on a felafel ball that has fallen to the ground at **Machaneh Yehudah**, the outdoor market. The spices make Zahava sneeze.

Labriut! Bless you!

They buzz straight to the **Biblical Zoo**. At Noah's Ark, they hop on a train that winds its way alongside bears, elephants, and flamingos.

"**Tel Aviv** has lots of fun places, too," Zvuvi calls out. "Let's go there next."

5

# The ZigZag Jerusalem – Tel Aviv Highway

Zzzig…Zzzag. Zvuvi and Zahava zigzag their way from **Jerusalem** to **Tel Aviv** along the a curvy highway.

They zoom over the Crusader Church at the Israeli Arab town of **Abu Ghosh**.

"I smell hot chickpeas!" Zvuvi says, pointing to the restaurant famous for its hummus.

They lower themselves for a landing. SWAT!

"I'll get you next time!" shouts the chef.

Kids are climbing on the old tanks at the Armored Corps Museum at **Latrun**, where battles were fought during Israel's War of Independence. Hup two, hup two. Zvuvi marches and salutes.

But wait, what's that they hear?  A shofar blowing?
Crowds cheering at a soccer game?

"Loooook," exclaims Zvuvi.  "It's **Mini Israel**."

"WOW! A map that's come alive!" Zahava smiles.

Zvuvi and Zahava are hiding somewhere
in Mini Israel.

Can you find them?

Have you checked at the Coca Cola Factory?
Or the ski slopes of Mt. Hermon?
Maybe they're hiding at the Dome of the Rock?

"It's hot," Zahava says. Zvuvi leads her inside the cool wonderland of **Soreq Cave**. "Those are stalactites," he says, pointing to the icicles hanging from the ceiling. "For thousands of years, water full of minerals drip, drip, dripped — and turned into stone. The icicles standing up are called stalagmites. Some formations have names such as The Ice Cream Cone or Snow White and the Seven Dwarfs." Uh, oh. Zvuvi has disappeared.

Can you find him?

The **Maccabean Village** at **Modi'in** is their next stop. "This is where Judah Maccabee lived," Zahava explains. "In the fall, you can help with the olive harvest. And on Hanukkah there is a torch parade."

"Look down!," Zvuvi says, as they soar over **Neot Kedumim**, the landscape reserve. Kids are eating a breakfast right out of the Bible— wheat, barley, figs, pomegranates, olives, grapes and date honey— the seven species found in Israel. Yummm.

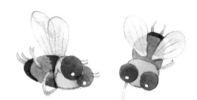

Zvuvi zooms in for a landing.

He zooms out again. Whew! Another close one.

# Tel Aviv – The City that Never Stops

Zvuvi is a city fly. He loves **Tel Aviv**. "Let's start with a roller coaster ride at **Luna Park**," he suggests.

"You're a roller coaster," Zahava insists, watching him zoom up and down.

On the boardwalk at the port, children whiz by on skateboards and bikes.

"Let's hop a ride," suggests Zvuvi, landing on a little girl's head. When she puts on her hat, Zvuvi ducks — just in time.

Spinning around, he hears the PING of a small black ball.

"ZVUVI! Come play matkot," shouts Zahava.

"This is fun," he agrees.

They fly over **Dizengoff Center** with its colorful water fountain. "Beautiful," flutters Zahava.

Then they soar up over the **Azrielli Towers** to **Ramat Gan**. "It looks like New York," Zahava says.

In **Safari Park**, lions roam, hippos splash, and monkeys jump on the car roofs. Children wave from pedal boats.

"Let's cross the street to **Ha'yarkon Park**. Those barbeques smell delicious." Zvuvi says.

Can you find Zvuvi at the park?

# Along the Coast

After lunch, Zvuvi and Zahava head north to visit family living along the coast.

"What shall we do first?" wonders Zvuvi. "Paraglide," he decides. "The wind is just right at **Netanya**. And, if anyone knows how to fly, it's us."

There's nothing fishy about their visit to Uncle Yanush at **Kibbutz Ma'ayan Zvi**. They find their cousins Avi, Benny, and Tal perched on a long pole, watching people fish. The fisherman swings the rod back. "Look out!" Zvuvi warns.

"Don't worry," Uncle Yanush calls. "This fisherman wouldn't hurt a fly."

SPLASH! Into the water they go.

Zvuvi and Zahava stop to visit their Uncle Kobi, who is perched on top of an oak barrel in a winery at **Zichron Ya'aKov**. Zvuvi takes a deep breath, inhaling the wonderful aroma. "Can't let you get drunk," Uncle Kobi says.

"Let's fly over to **Dor Beach**," suggests Zvuvi. "It's the calmest in all of Israel. If you build a sand castle, it will stay in place for days."

As Zahava finishes digging a moat, Zvuvi announces, "Time for the concert at the amphitheater."

"The what theater?" Zahava's never heard that word.

"The outdoor theater that King Herod built 2000 years ago in the ancient Roman city of **Caesarea**," Zvuvi answers her.

They soar over headless statues and take their seats.

# Haifa and its Layers

Ship Ahoy! Zvuvi puts on his captain's hat and he and Zahava board a boat for a cruise along **Haifa's** coast. The ship glides past the **Maritime Museum**. "You can learn all about shipbuilding there," says Zvuvi.

The boat docks near the aerial cable car. From the window they have a fly's eye view. Riding up, up, up, they reach the top of **Mount Carmel** and the old **Stella Maris Lighthouse**.

"I wish we were fireflies," teases Zvuvi. "We could signal Elijah in his cave down below."

They fly from hilltop to hilltop playing "peak-a-boo," and discover how the city is built into many layers of the mountain.

"Awesome!" Zvuvi says, looking at the gleaming gold dome of the **Bahai Shrine.** They swoop down and land among emerald green lawns, beautifully cut bushes, and stone peacocks and eagles.

Can you find Zvuvi at the gardens?

"Wow! So may steps!" Zahava exclaims.

15

# Galloping in the Galilee

Yippee-Yi-Yay! Visiting a **Horse Ranch** is perfect for a dude like Zvuvi.

The horse swats him with his tail.

"Let's go see some of the farms up north," says Zahava.

"I'll find you one that's busy as a bee," Zvuvi says. They follow the buzz to **Dvorat Hatavor**, a silk and honey farm at the foot of Mount Tavor. A farmer tells a group of tourists that silk and honey are made the same way as they were made in Biblical times.

Zvuvi and Zehava watch the silkworms sway back and forth. They're making small silk cocoons to hide in. After awhile, they'll change into silk moths.

Next they fly to the dairy farm on **Moshav Beit Hillel**. Visitors can help milk the cows. "I'm going to milk a brown one," says Zvuvi, "so that we can have chocolate milk."

Now answer this: Which country has the cow breed that gives the most milk?

Israel—with its Holstein cows

"Now grab your pail and let's head to the Druze village of **Peki'in** where we can fill it up with olives," Zvuvi orders.

A beautifully dressed sheikh is sitting in his courtyard. Something itches. The sheikh starts to scratch. Suddenly he slaps his belly. Oh, oh. Zvuvi better watch it.

# Action in the Upper Galilee

Zvuvi is a daredevil! He leads Zahava to the cable cars at **Manara Cliffs** and helps her buckle her seatbelt.

"Now I'm going to zipline down the cliff," he tells her when they get to the top. "You can take a hike!"

Zvuvi grabs on to a boy in a harness and ZIP. . . . down they go. "Wheeee . . . this is fun!"

Zahava can't keep track of him.

Can you help her find Zvuvi?

For more adventure, Zvuvi heads to **Kfar Blum** to kayak down the **Jordan River**. He hops into a raft with some teenagers. The boys hold their paddles over their heads so they don't catch on the rocks.

"Bop, bop," Zvuvi says, as they zoom down the rapids.

"You know I can't hear you with the water rushing," Zahava answers. "Just be careful you don't tip over."

# Skating, Skiing, and Hiking Up North

Ice skating and skiing in the summer? Is Mother Nature playing tricks? The cousins are on their way to **Metulla**, a small town at the tippy top of Israel.

Zvuvi heads to the ice skating rink at **Canada Center**. Two skaters glide by.

"They're training for the Olympics," he tells Zahava.

"Let's go skiing on **Mt. Hermon**," he urges Zahava, heading to Israel's only ski slope.

"Not me," she insists, as Zvuvi straps on a pair of skis.

"You're such a 'fraidy fly,'" he teases. "You take the chairlift. I'll be back."

Can you track Zvuvi?

He lands at the foot of the mountain at the beautiful **Banias waterfall**. Water crashes over the rocks, spraying Zahava.

"I love nature," she admits. "At the **Hula Reserve** you can find migrating cranes, storks, and pelicans on their way from Africa to Europe."

"That place is for the birds," Zvuvi shrugs.

# Round and Round the Kinneret

Zvuvi and Zahava have decided to hitch a bike ride around **Lake Kinneret**.

They hold tight as the bikers pedal to **Tiberias** where the Jerusalem Talmud was written hundreds of years ago. At the **Dana Gracia Hotel Museum,** they try on fun costumes from VERY long ago.

Zvuvi sniffs. "Something's fishy." Grilled St. Peter's Fish, freshly caught for lunch! Uh, oh. Here comes the cook.

Zvuvi flees.

SMACK!

The bikers decide to cool off at **Dugit Beach.** "Yipee!" Zahava cries. "I can go on the water slide at **Luna Gal Water Park.**"

*Can you find her?*

Zvuvi prefers taking a lazy boat ride on the lake, but they need to hurry up because the bikers are leaving.

Zahava wants to relax at the Roman Baths at **Hamat Gader**. Suddenly she screeches, "Maybe this is NOT for me!"

"It's for me!" Zvuvi beams, bouncing on the back of an alligator at the **Alligator Farm**.

"GOTCHA," one snaps, opening his mouth wide. But Zvuvi is too fast.

# Heading South

"Isn't there a spa without alligators?" Zahava asks Zvuvi.

"The **Dead Sea** — it's one of the world's first health spas," he offers.

"I'm not going any place that's not alive," she insists.

"It will make you come alive," explains Zvuvi.

"But first let's stop at **Qumran**. Remember that mushroom-shaped museum in Jerusalem with all the Dead Sea Scrolls? They were found here hidden in jars."

"NEAT," says Zahava.

Zvuvi's hiding.
Can you find him?

As they glide across the brown desert rock, they see a burst of green and hear the sound of rushing water. "Are we at the spa?" asks Zahava.

"Nope." Zvuvi points to a sign: Welcome to the **Ein Gedi Nature Reserve**. A cute little ibex runs by. The flies follow the sounds of giggling children to a waterfall, and join them under the cool spray.

welcome to the Ein Gedi Nature Reserve

"Ready to get wet?" Zvuvi asks.

Zahava puts her leg down. "No. I want to get to the spa."

25

# Taking it Easy at the Dead Sea

Off they fly. On the way, they pass over the famous fortress at **Mount Masada**. "We can take the cable car or climb the snake path to the top," Zvuvi suggests.

"NO," insists Zahava. "The spa. NOW!"

Zvuvi obeys.

As they reach the **Dead Sea** they see a man floating on his back, reading a newspaper.

"WOW!" exclaims Zahava. "How does he do that?"

"The water is heavy," Zvuvi explains. "It's full of salt and minerals."

"Here's mud in your face!" Zvuvi laughs as he massages something wet and sticky onto Zahava's cheeks. "Did you know this is the lowest place on earth?" he asks her.

# A Crater Meeting at Mitzpe Ramon

A hot breeze carries Zvuvi and Zahava across the **Negev's** desert to the Air Force Museum at **Hatzerim**. Sooo many planes! Zvuvi is pretending to be a pilot.

Can you find him in the cockpit?

"That old wooden plane is called The Mosquito," Zvuvi whispers. "Maybe one of these days they'll name a plane after us."

It's market day in **Be'er Sheva**. Bedouins have come from nearby villages to buy and sell camels.

"SNORT."

"Is that you, Zvuvi?" Zahava asks.

"I'm talking to the camels," he says, "and I'm thinking that maybe we should . . ."

"Uh oh," sighs Zahava.

". . . ride one."

They hop on a tall, friendly camel.

"This is a bumpy ride," sighs Zahava.

They wind their way through the dry, sandy roads to the deep, colorful crater at **Mitzpe Ramon**.

"It's huge!" exclaims Zahava.

"And we're going to go all the way to the bottom in a jeep," beams Zvuvi.

"First a camel, now a jeep . . . what next?" Zahava asks.

"Alpacas and llamas," winks Zvuvi, "and we have lots of relatives at the farm."

# A Lot of Fun in Eilat

"I want to swim with the dolphins," says Zvuvi. So off they fly to **Eilat**.

Passing over the copper mines at **Timna Park**, they see the famous Timna Mushroom made from pink sandstone.

"OUCH, it's hot," screams Zahava.

Finally they land at the Red Sea. Zahava starts a water fight with Zvuvi. He splashes back so hard, he somersaults through the air.

Can you track them?

Whooosh. . . . Zvuvi lands. They glide with the scuba divers in wet suits and masks to the sea floor, through beautiful coral reefs, and dozens of tropical fish and underwater plants. Blub, blub, blub.

Zvuvi waves to the tourists peeking through the portholes of the **Yellow Submarine**.

They've reached the **Dolphin Reef**.

Can you find Zvuvi?

Welcome to Dolphin Ree

A tired Zahava decides to head for home. Full of energy, Zvuvi
is ready for more adventure.

"Shalom, Zvuvi," calls Zahava, waving to her cousin.

"Shalom, Zahava," he waves back.

Where do you think Zvuvi will go next? We'll have to wait and see.

"Lehitraot — See you soon!" calls Zvuvi.

# Lehitraot, Zvuvi!

 ## Did you find Zvuvi and Zahava?

Is it too cold for flies on the ski slope at **Mini-Israel** (p. 7)?

Check out Snow White and the Seven Dwarfs at the **Soreq Caves** (p. 8).

Let's hope the hippo at **Safari Park** (p. 11) doesn't close his mouth.

Look up into the palm trees at the **Bahai Gardens** (p. 15).

Look under the cable car in the center of the page at **Manara Cliffs** (p. 18).

He's coming around the slopes on **Mt. Hermon** (p. 20).

Wheee! Zahava is about to get wet at **Dugit Beach** (p. 22)!

At the **Qumran Caves** (p. 24) Zvuvi's hiding in a hole . . . on the left.

Check all the blue planes at the **Air Force Museum** (p. 28).

Let's hope they don't get too close to the coral in **Eilat** (p. 30).

Someone we know is riding high at the **Dolphin Reef** (p. 31).